THE FARMER IN THE DELL

A Singing Game

Pictures by
Mary Maki Rae

Viking Kestrel

VIKING KESTREL
Published by the Penguin Group
Viking Penguin Inc., 40 West 23rd Street, New York, New York 10010, U.S.A.
Penguin Books Ltd, 27 Wrights Lane, London W8 5TZ England
Penguin Books Australia Ltd, Ringwood, Victoria, Australia
Penguin Books Canada Ltd, 2801 John Street, Markham, Ontario, Canada L3R 1B4
Penguin Books (N.Z.) Ltd, 182–190 Wairau Road, Auckland 10, New Zealand

Penguin Books Ltd, Registered Offices: Harmondsworth, Middlesex, England

First published in 1988 by Viking Penguin Inc.
Published simultaneously in Canada
Copyright © Mary Maki Rae, 1988
All rights reserved
The musical arrangement of "The Farmer in the Dell" on page 26 used by permission of
The American Heritage Publishing Company

Library of Congress Cataloging-in-Publication Data
Rae, Mary Maki.   The farmer in the dell.
Summary: This illustrated edition includes the entire song with music and ideas for playing this traditional game.
1. Nursery rhymes, American.   2. Children's poetry, American.   3. Folk-songs—United States.   4. Children's songs—United
States. [1. Nursery rhymes.   2. Folk songs, American.   3. Singing games.   4. Games] I. Title.
PZ8.3.R122Far   1988   [E]   87-31799
ISBN 0-670-81853-4

Color separations by Imago Ltd., Hong Kong
Printed in Hong Kong by South China Printing Company
Set in Cheltenham Book
1   2   3   4   5   92   91   90   89   88

*To all
buoyant,
light-hearted
children
of the future,
past,
and present*

The farmer in the dell,
The farmer in the dell,
Heigh-ho, the derry-o,
The farmer in the dell.

The farmer takes a wife,
The farmer takes a wife,
Heigh-ho, the derry-o,
The farmer takes a wife.

The wife takes a child,
The wife takes a child,
Heigh-ho, the derry-o,
The wife takes a child.

The child takes a nurse,
The child takes a nurse,
Heigh-ho, the derry-o,
The child takes a nurse.

The nurse takes a dog,
The nurse takes a dog,
Heigh-ho, the derry-o,
The nurse takes a dog.

The dog takes a cat,
The dog takes a cat,
Heigh-ho, the derry-o,
The dog takes a cat.

The cat takes a rat,
The cat takes a rat,
Heigh-ho, the derry-o,
The cat takes a rat.

The rat takes a cheese,
The rat takes a cheese,
Heigh-ho, the derry-o,
The rat takes a cheese.

The cheese stands alone!
The cheese stands alone!
Heigh-ho, the derry-o,
The cheese stands alone!

THE FARMER IN THE DELL

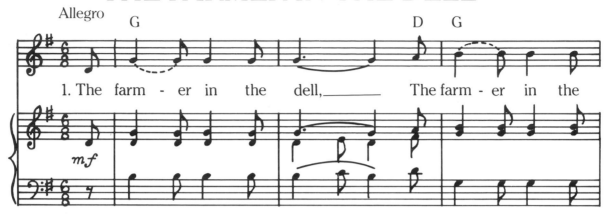

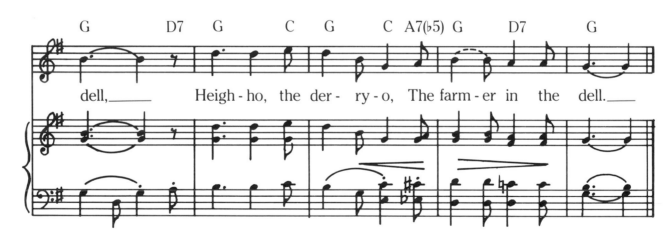

2. The farmer takes a wife,
   The farmer takes a wife,
   Heigh-ho, the derry-o,
   The farmer takes a wife.

3. The wife takes a child, *etc.*

4. The child takes a nurse, *etc.*

5. The nurse takes a dog, *etc.*

6. The dog takes a cat, *etc.*

7. The cat takes a rat, *etc.*

8. The rat takes a cheese, *etc.*

9. The cheese stands alone! *etc.*

ABOUT THIS BOOK

"The Farmer in the Dell" is the best known of the many singing games that originated in the Middle Ages. It was originally called "The Farmer's in his Den." (The Old English *denn* refers to a clearing in the woods—just as *dell*, in the American, British, and Australian versions, is a hollow surrounded by trees.) It was a functional part of social life, in which young people could declare preferences for each other within the safe, formal framework of a game.

The game arrived in America in 1883, as part of the culture of the West German immigrants. But circle dances actually have evolved from as far back as the ancient world of 1350 B.C. The beginning of sculptural art—exemplified by Cretan pottery—depicts men and women with hands joined in a ring dance. Homer describes a ring dance in a scene in *The Iliad* c. 800 B.C. And, at the time of Jesus, the choosing of a sweetheart from a dancing ring of maidens was a popular custom.

"The Farmer in the Dell" game is best played in a big space. All join hands and encircle one player who is the "farmer." The farmer (with eyes open or closed) chooses one player from the circle to be his wife—or her husband—and he or she joins the farmer in the center of the ring.

The wife then selects the child, the child chooses a nurse, and so on as each verse is sung, ending with the cheese. These players may join hands to form a circle in the middle, turning in the opposite direction from the outer circle.

Once the cheese is selected, all players join hands with the outer ring again, encircling the cheese who then becomes the farmer—and the game begins again.